THE BEST, BEST, BEST BABY!

ANTHEA SIMMONS **GEORGIE BIRKETT**

ANDERSEN PRESS

My little brother's still pretty new
And there's still lots of stuff
that he can't do.

He can't really run
And he can't climb trees!

He can't say "thank you"
And he can't say "please"!

He can't dress himself.
He can't choose his clothes!

He can't brush his teeth

And he can't blow his nose!

He can't draw a picture

But he **CAN** make a mess
And he can throw food

And he can stick his
tongue out
And be very rude!

And he can get very dirty

YAAA

AAAAAH!

And he can scream and shout.

And "Me!"

and "cake"

and "out!"

He can get up too early.
He can keep me awake.

He can break my toys sometimes
(Mum says it's by mistake).

And when I'm getting grumpy
And wish he wasn't there

He smiles his special
baby smile

And tugs on my hair.

And stares at my face.

He holds on tightly to my hand

And that's when I know that no-one can take his place.

And even though there's lots of stuff
That makes me cross or sad.

He's still the best, BEST baby brother

That a sister ever had.